This book belongs to:

_____

_____

Berryland Books

Written by Gill Davies
Illustrated by Eric Kincaid
Edited by Heather Maddock

Published by Berryland Books
www.berrylandbooks.com

First published in 2004

ISBN 1-84577-002-1
Printed in India

The Emperor's New Clothes

Reading should always be FUN !

Reading is one of the most important skills your child will learn. It's an exciting challenge that you can enjoy together.

Treasured Tales is a collection of stories that has been carefully written for young readers.

Here are some useful points to help you teach your child to read.

Try to set aside a regular quiet time for reading at least three times a week.

Choose a time of the day when your child is not too tired.

Plan to spend approximately 15 minutes on each session.

Select the book together and spend the first few minutes talking about the title and cover picture.

Spend the next ten minutes listening and encouraging your child to read.

Always allow your child to look at and use the pictures to help them with the story.

Spend the last couple of minutes asking your child about what they have read. You will find a few examples of questions at the bottom of some pages.

Understanding what they have read is as important as the reading itself.

There was once a rich Emperor who liked his clothes very much.

Infact, he wore a new outfit every day.

"Tell my tailors to make me some new shirts straight away," he would say to his servants.

"I want a new hat and a smart new cloak for tomorrow," he would continue.

"How I like to wear new clothes," he would say.

How often does the Emperor change his clothes?

One day two new tailors arrived at the palace and asked to see the Emperor.

"Oh Emperor," said the tailors, "your clothes are indeed very fine, but so out of fashion.

We can weave the finest cloth you have ever seen and you will look better than you have ever looked before," they said.

"Really," said the Emperor "that sounds very interesting and tell me, what is so special about this cloth?"

The two tailors bowed again, smiling to themselves.

"The magic cloth we weave is so fine and so beautiful that only clever people can see it," said the first tailor.

"You will be able to judge who is wise and who is stupid," said the second.

Who will be able to see the cloth?

"Amazing," said the Emperor.

"I should like you to make me a new suit at once," he said.

The Emperor then gave the tailors a big bag of gold coins to pay for the cloth.

As soon as the tailors stepped outside the palace they began to laugh and jump with joy.

"The Emperor is so easily fooled!" they said to each other.

These two men were not tailors and nothing they had said was true.

The two men set up looms and pretended to weave.

A few days later the Emperor called for the Prime Minister and asked him to go and see how the cloth was coming along.

The Prime Minister went to the tailors and asked to have a look.

"Of course, come in and see the most beautiful cloth you have ever seen," the tailors said.

The Prime Minister could not see a thing!

Could the Prime Minister see the cloth?

He returned to the palace and went to see the Emperor.

Not wanting to appear stupid in front of the Emperor he said, "The cloth is the most beautiful I have ever seen."

The Emperor was very pleased.

Soon after, the Emperor sent his family to look at the cloth.

They too could not see the magic cloth, but did not want to seem stupid.

"Amazing," they told the Emperor.

The lords and ladies went to see the cloth.

"Look how fine it is," said the naughty tailors.

"Look at the gold thread and how beautifully it falls," they continued.

The lords and ladies could not see a thing and stared at the empty loom.

"The cloth is indeed wonderful, the Emperor will be very pleased," one of the lords said, not wanting to appear stupid.

Everyone agreed.

Who went to see the cloth?

At last the Emperor wanted to see this marvellous cloth for himself.

He stood beside the empty loom and rubbed his eyes.

"Have you ever seen such beautiful cloth?" the wicked tailors said to the Emperor.

The Emperor did not want to appear stupid, after all, everyone else had seen the cloth.

"It is indeed the most beautiful I have ever seen," the Emperor replied.

The Emperor then left, giving another bag of gold coins to the tailors.

Finally, the day came for the Emperor to try on his new suit.

The tailors fussed around, pretending to dress the Emperor.

"Perfect, don't you think?" they said aloud to each other.

What were the tailors pretending to do?

The Emperor stood in front of his mirror.

He couldn't see a thing!

"Perfect," said the Emperor, "The cloth is so fine that it feels like I'm wearing nothing at all!"

The tailors stood still, trying not to laugh.

The Emperor called his family and all the lords and ladies to come and admire his new suit.

They were all surprised to see the Emperor standing there with nothing on.

No one could see the magic suit.

No one wanted to appear stupid.

"What a wonderful suit!" someone said.

"Marvellous!" said another.

"So beautiful!" said a third.

The Emperor was so pleased he decided to wear his new suit for his birthday parade the very next day.

The following day the Emperor climbed up into his golden coach.

Everyone had gathered to see his amazing new suit.

They cheered, clapped and pretended
to be able to see the suit.

Could anyone see the suit?

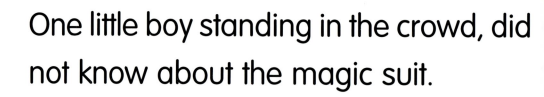

One little boy standing in the crowd, did not know about the magic suit.

He looked at the Emperor and shouted "The Emperor has nothing on, he's naked!"

All at once, everyone started to shout "The Emperor is naked!"

The Emperor realized he had been fooled and returned to the palace as quickly as he could.

The naughty tailors were nowhere to be found.

They had left the palace, taking the gold coins and never returned again!